W9-BVM-396

This book belongs to:

Timmy Tricinelli

Spooky Nights

By Gail Herman

Illustrated by Duendes del Sur

ADVANCE PUBLISHERS

SCOOBY-DOO!

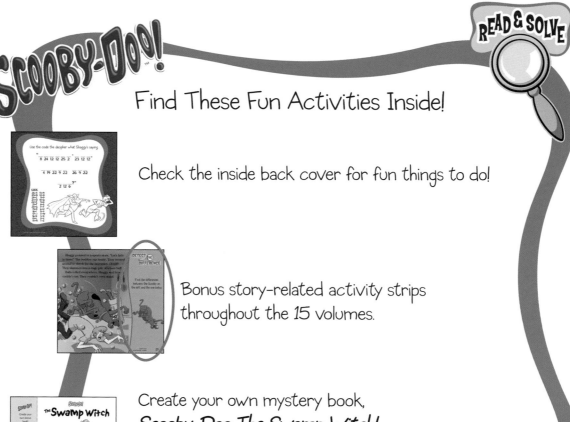

READ & SOLVE

Find These Fun Activities Inside!

Check the inside back cover for fun things to do!

Bonus story-related activity strips throughout the 15 volumes.

Create your own mystery book,
Scooby-Doo The Swamp Witch!
Color, collect, and staple the coloring pages
at the end of the first 12 books in
the Scooby-Doo Read & Solve mystery series.

Advance PUBLISHERS

www.advancepublishers.com
Produced by Judy O Productions, Inc.
Designed by SunDried Penguin Design
All rights reserved.
Printed in China

The Mystery Machine bumped along a dark, empty road.

Scooby-Doo and his friends bumped along, too.

"Like, we're in the middle of nowhere!" said Shaggy. "I hope we have enough gas!"

COUNTING MYSTERY

How many times does the vampire appear in this book?

3

All at once, the van stopped.

"Roh-oh!" said Scooby.

"Zoinks!" said Shaggy. "We *are* out of gas!"

"No," said Fred. He checked under the hood.
"Engine trouble. We have to call a tow truck."

Velma and Daphne looked around. Where could they find a telephone?

"Rook!" Scooby cried. He pointed down the road.

"I hope it's a house," Velma said, "so we can use the phone."

"And the fridge," Shaggy added.

The gang walked toward the light.
The light grew brighter.

They were getting closer.
Suddenly, Velma said, "Jinkies!
It's not a house. It's a castle!"

The castle looked spooky.

Scooby dug in his paws. He didn't want to move.

"Come on, old buddy," Shaggy said. "Think fridge!"

In a flash, Scooby swam across the moat. He banged on the drawbridge with his tail.

The drawbridge dropped.
Suits of armor stood at the door.
"Cool statues," said Shaggy.
Clank, clank. The helmets snapped open.
They weren't suits of armor. They were
knights. Shiny spooky knights!

"Who goes there?" one knight cried.
"Nobody," cried Shaggy. He and Scooby
backed away.

"Come on," said Fred. "We have to find a phone."
Scooby shook his head. "Ro way."
"For a Scooby Snack?" Velma said.
Shaggy and Scooby raced inside.

MYSTERY MIX-UP?

Unscramble the letters to solve these word mysteries.

ucmotes

rpyta

ctiwh

ummym

otemnsr

sohtg

Inside the castle, a chandelier swung back and forth.

Creak, creak.

"That's funny," said Daphne. "There's no breeze. What is making it move?"

"Rhosts!" Scooby whispered to Shaggy.

12

"Ghosts?" Shaggy said as a strange man rushed into the room.

The man opened his mouth to speak. Scooby stared at his sharp, pointy teeth.

"Rangs!" said Scooby.

"He's a vampire!" Shaggy cried.

Shaggy and Scooby ran.
But the vampire ran, too.

"Like, since we're running," Shaggy said,
"let's run to the kitchen."
"Reah!" said Scooby.

In the kitchen, they saw a woman. She
stirred a giant pot that bubbled over a fire.
"A witch!" cried Shaggy.

"You two are perfect!" said the witch.
"Just what I need."

"No way," said Shaggy. "We're not part of your spooky recipe!"

Find the chain on this
page, and then find
four more on
the following pages.

Shaggy and Scooby raced away.
"Stop!" cried the witch.
"Stop!" cried the vampire.
They chased Shaggy and Scooby down
the stairs, to a dark, dark dungeon!

18

Answer: one on page 19,
one on page 20, two on page 28.

Shaggy and Scooby backed into the corner.

Suddenly, a mummy leaped up.

"Time is up!" he shouted.

"Our time is up, Scoob," Shaggy cried.

"We've got to get out of here!"

19

They raced up the stairs.
"Stop!" cried the mummy.
"Stop!" cried the witch.

"Stop!" cried the vampire.
"Let's find Velma, Fred, and Daphne.
Then we'll get out of here," said Shaggy.

Finally, Shaggy flung open a door.
Down below, they saw monsters
and zombies and ghosts. . . .

And Velma, Daphne, and Fred!
A knight stood over them. He held
his sword tight.

"What should we do?" Shaggy asked Scooby.

Just then the vampire, witch, and mummy leaped beside them.

"Rump!" said Scooby.

"Jump?" Shaggy yelled. Shaggy grabbed
the chandelier.
Scooby grabbed Shaggy.
They swung across the room.

Shaggy and Scooby dropped to the floor —
right on top of the knight!

"My sword!" the knight cried.

"Grab it, Fred!" Shaggy shouted.

Fred scooped it up. But then
he gave it back to the knight!

Scooby hid his eyes. He was afraid to look. "Relax," Velma said. "The knight is going to cut the cake."

DETECT THE DIFFERENCE

Find the differences between Scooby on this page and the one below.

Answer: missing spots on arm, missing SD on tag, pads on paws are different colors

Velma stepped out of the way. Now Shaggy could see a party cake!
"It's a costume party!" Velma said.
"But," said Shaggy, "what about the ghostly chandelier?"

"I was pulling a string," said the vampire, "to move the chandelier into place."

"And the witch's potion?" Shaggy asked.

"Punch!" said the witch. "I wanted you to try it."

"And the mummy's warning, 'Time is up'?"

The mummy smiled. "My nap time was over!"

"But you chased us!" said Shaggy.

"Sure," said the vampire, "to invite you to the party."

"Uh, we knew it all along, right, Scoob?" said Shaggy.

"We were just acting."

Scooby looked around at all the smiling faces.
He stood up and bowed. "Scooby-Dooby Doo!"

"Would you like to use the phone now?" asked the knight.
"Uh, no rush," said Shaggy. "How about some cake?"

Match Fred to his correct shadow.

1.

2.

3.

4.

Help Shaggy putt his way to the 18th hole.

START

RIP

FINISH